DISCARDED

NO THUMPIN', NO BUMPIN',
NO RUMPUS TONIGHT!

NO THUMPIN', NO BUMPIN', NO RUMPUS TONIGHT!

NANCY PATZ

Atheneum   1990   New York

Atheneum
Macmillan Publishing Company
866 Third Avenue, New York, NY 10022
Collier Macmillan Canada, Inc.
First Edition
Printed in Singapore
10   9   8   7   6   5   4   3   2   1

Library of Congress Cataloging-in-Publication Data
Patz, Nancy.
No thumpin', no bumpin', no rumpus tonight! / written and illustrated by
Nancy Patz.   p.   cm.
Summary: Late one night Benjamin and Elephant secretly prepare a
very special breakfast for Benjamin's mother's birthday.
ISBN 0-689-31510-4
[1. Breakfast—Fiction.   2. Birthdays—Fiction.   3. Humorous
stories.]   I. Title.
PZ7.P27833Nm 1990   [E]—dc19
88-7717   CIP   AC

To my daughters
JEANNE PATZ BLAUSTEIN
SUSAN BLAUSTEIN BERLOW

Late one dark and quiet night, long before the sun came up, everybody was asleep—except...

Benjamin and Elephant. They were busy as usual.

"Hey, El," said Benjamin, "today's my mother's birthday! Let's make breakfast and surprise her."

"You bet, Benj!" said Elephant.

"We've got a great big breakfast to fix, and Mom gets up at quarter of six—so hurry, El! And remember, be quiet! No rumpus, all right?"

"No thumpin', no bumpin', no rumpus tonight! You can count on *me,* Benj!" Elephant whispered.

"I make terrific cereal," said Elephant. "First I mash a macaroni with a slice of nice baloney, add a drop of soda pop and then a glop of ketchup and…"

"Ketchup in cereal?" asked Benjamin.

"Ketchup makes it *pretty*, Benj," said Elephant.

"Then I plunk a hunk of cheese! Mush the mustard!
Pour the peas! Add some rice, and then for spice I think
we need some pickle juice...."

"Pickle juice in cereal?"

"It peps it up!" said Elephant.

"This cereal needs peanuts," said Elephant,
and he poked around for peanuts. But he
grabbed peanut *butter* by mistake and lost his
balance completely!

"*Watch it,* El!" yelled Benjamin.

But Elephant stumbled! *Thumpitty-BUMP!*

Shelves shook and jars jiggled and *BAM!* the door
slammed tight!

"I told you, El, no rumpus tonight! You'll get us in plenty of
trouble, for sure! Look at the clock—it's ten after four!"

"Sorry, Benj," said Elephant. But then he got a great idea.

"Where's the jelly?" he whispered....

"Here's the yellow jelly—or would you like the red?"

"Red spreads better, Benj."

"Red spreads better?"

"Right! Red spreads better, 'cause red's a better spreader, so the bread's spread better with the red!"

Benjamin laughed. "Oh, El, you're silly!"

"But I'm such a good cook! Watch *this*!" said Elephant.
Up like a rainbow over his head he tossed the peanut-buttered bread and spread it all with jelly. Everything went fine until...
"*Look out,* El!"

Oranges, oranges—seventeen oranges!—bounced and bobbled across the floor. Suddenly Benjamin's mother called from down the hall!

"WHAT'S GOING ON IN THERE, BENJAMIN?"

Benjamin looked at the clock on the wall.

"Nothing, Mom!" he shouted.

"Well, get back to bed right away!" she said.

"I told you, be quiet!" Benjamin scolded.

"We've still got lots of things to fix, and Mom gets up at quarter of six."

"No rumpus, I promise!" Elephant whispered.

But…

he fiddled around with an orange—and got a great idea.

"Want fresh juice for breakfast, Benj?"

"Sure," said Benjamin. "Where's the juice?"

Elephant just giggled….

"Watch *this*!" he said. And he scooped up an orange
and gave it a squeeze till juice shot out like a rocket.

Benjamin laughed. "Let's see you do that again!"

He wound up and fired a fast ball.

Elephant caught it *plunk!* in his trunk and squished the juice
high into the air.

"Play ball, Benj! Put it right there!"

And Benjamin did. He pitched the orange with all his might.
Elephant yelled, "NO RUMPUS TONIGHT!"—and missed the
pitch by a mile.
"Here comes a knuckleball!" Benjamin warned....

But Elephant nabbed it with a mighty dive.
The clock on the wall said 4:55.
　　Then Benjamin tried a change of pace—and
Elephant tripped in a slippery place and slid in
the slush across the floor!

They both laughed hard, and Benjamin called, "Get *this*, El!"
He threw a curve that plopped in the drink. And then a knuckleball
that bounced in the sink!

But Elephant saved it with a double play: he caught the orange
and drank the spray!

"Just a couple more, El. I bet it's getting late!"

The clock on the wall said 5:08.

But Benjamin looped one way too high. Elephant leaped to catch
the fly, and he…

walloped the pots on the wall with his trunk—and the pots all crashed to the floor. They clanked. They clinked. They clattered. They clunked. And, oh, how they flashed as they clashed in the splash of the cool, bright orange juice light!

"NO RUMPUS! NO THUMPUS! NO...

"BUMPUS TONIGHT!" Elephant roared.

Benjamin hollered, "QUIET! BE QUIET! I'm telling you, Elephant, IF YOU'RE NOT QUIET—"

But, *then,* just then...

Benjamin's mother's angry voice was right outside
the kitchen door!
"BENJAMIN! WHAT ARE YOU *DOING* IN THERE?"

Benjamin dashed out into the hall.
"Everything's fine, Mom! You don't have to come in!"
"WHAT *ARE* YOU DOING? I WANT TO KNOW!"
He couldn't think of a thing to say.

Elephant whispered, "Say it's a surprise!"

"It's a *surprise,* Mom! Don't come in! Please, Mom—*please*?"

"*Well…*" said Benjamin's mother slowly. "*Well…*" At last she said, "Well, *all right,* Benjamin—but get back to bed right away!" And she turned around and went down the hall.

"*Whew!* That was close!" gasped Benjamin.

Elephant sighed. "I guess I forgot to be quiet."

"Elephants never forget, El."

"They do when they're having fun, Benj," said Elephant.

"We'd better get rid of this mess," said Benjamin.

Elephant nodded. "Just watch me clean!"

The clock on the wall said 5:15.

They put away the cereal,
soda pop and cheese…
sliced baloney, macaroni,
pickles, rice and peas.
Then ketchup. Then mustard.
   "We're practically done!"
   "*Keep working,* El!"
It was 5:21.

They cleaned off the countertop.
They mopped up the floor.
The clock on the wall said 5:34.

They wiped off the pitcher with
the orange juice in it.
   "*Hurry up,* El! There's only a
minute!"
   "Got the cups and dishes?"
   "Anything else to fix?"
The clock on the wall said sixteen
of six when quietly, quietly…

ever so quietly they tiptoed down the hall.

"HAPPY BIRTHDAY!" Benjamin shouted.
"Such a surprise!" His mother laughed....

"Mmmm…unusual cereal," she said. "It smells a bit like ketchup."

"I think it needs peanuts!" said Benjamin.

"You must have worked hard to squeeze all this juice," said his mother. Benjamin and Elephant winked at each other.

Then Benjamin's mother emptied her cup
as the night disappeared and the sun came up.

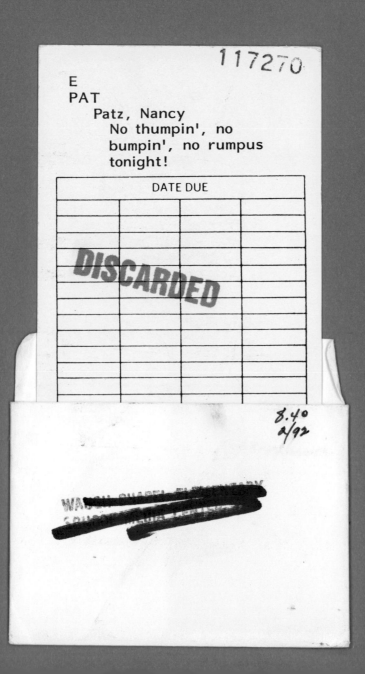

117270

E
PAT
   Patz, Nancy
     No thumpin', no
     bumpin', no rumpus
     tonight!

DATE DUE			

8.40
2/92

no bumpin', no rumpus tonig
3774812
Patz WAUGH CHAPEL ELEMENTARY